Sunny days

by
Jesse Byrd

Illustrated by Anastasiia Ku

"Let your light shine."
To the amazing family and friends who inspire me daily.

Sunny Days
Copyright © 2017 by Jesse Byrd Creative INC
All rights reserved.

ISBN: 978-0-9997050-0-1
10 9 8 7 6 5 4 3 2 1
Printed in the United States of America

MARTINE IS SKIPPING TO SCHOOL.

She stopped to peek inside of Mr. Pip's Bakery. His shop always smelled of delicious cupcakes, sprinkles and warm strawberry icing.

Pies

Cookies

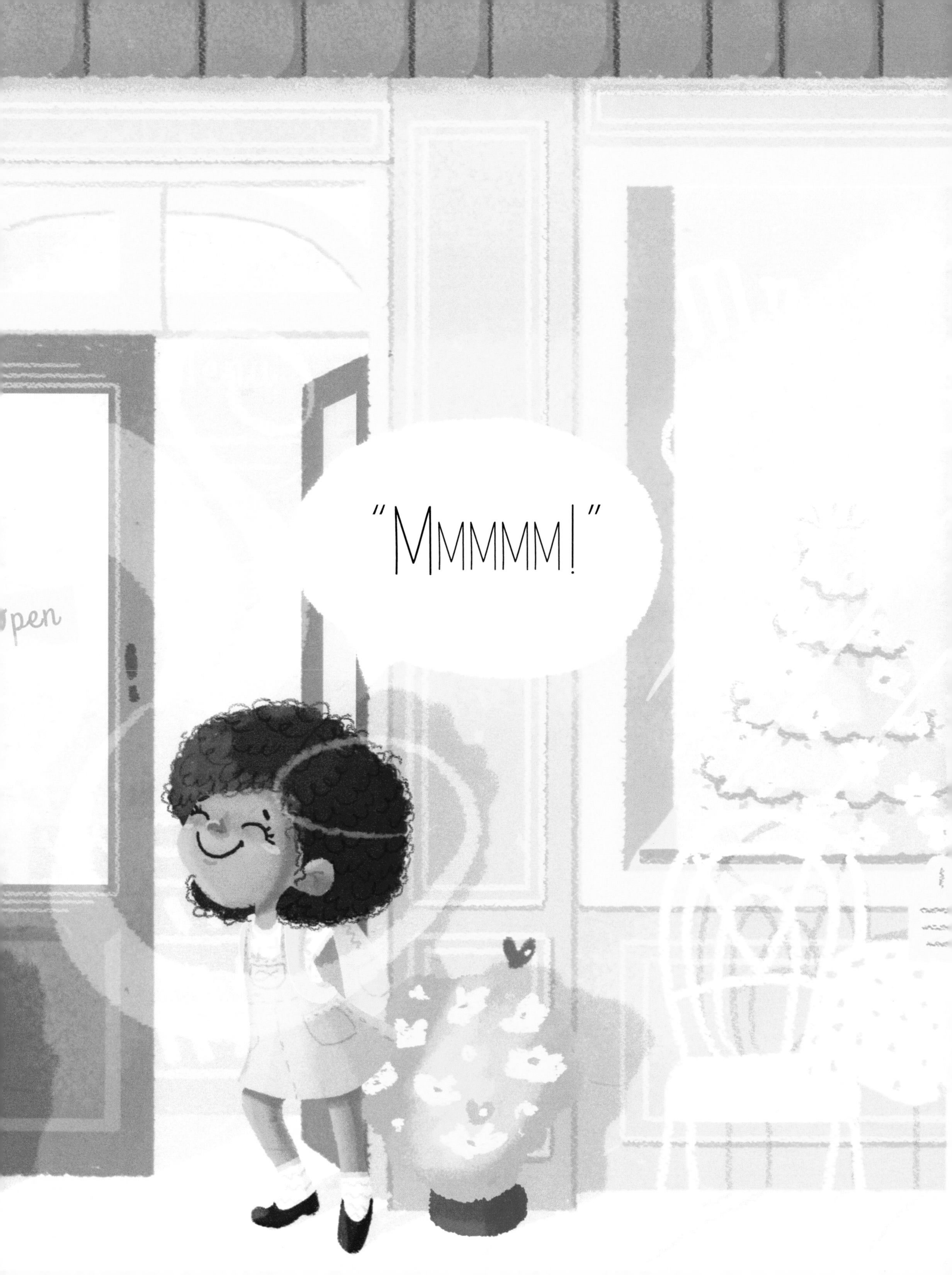
"Mmmmm!"

MR. PIP WAS SO SURPRISED HE NEARLY DROPPED HIS CAKE.

Next, Martine stopped at Ms. Shirley's Music Studio. Ms. Shirley's students played the most beautiful music you could ever hear. Sometimes, they would come outside and play songs for the whole neighborhood! People would rush out of their homes and shops carrying fancy umbrellas and dance in the street! Everyone loved it!

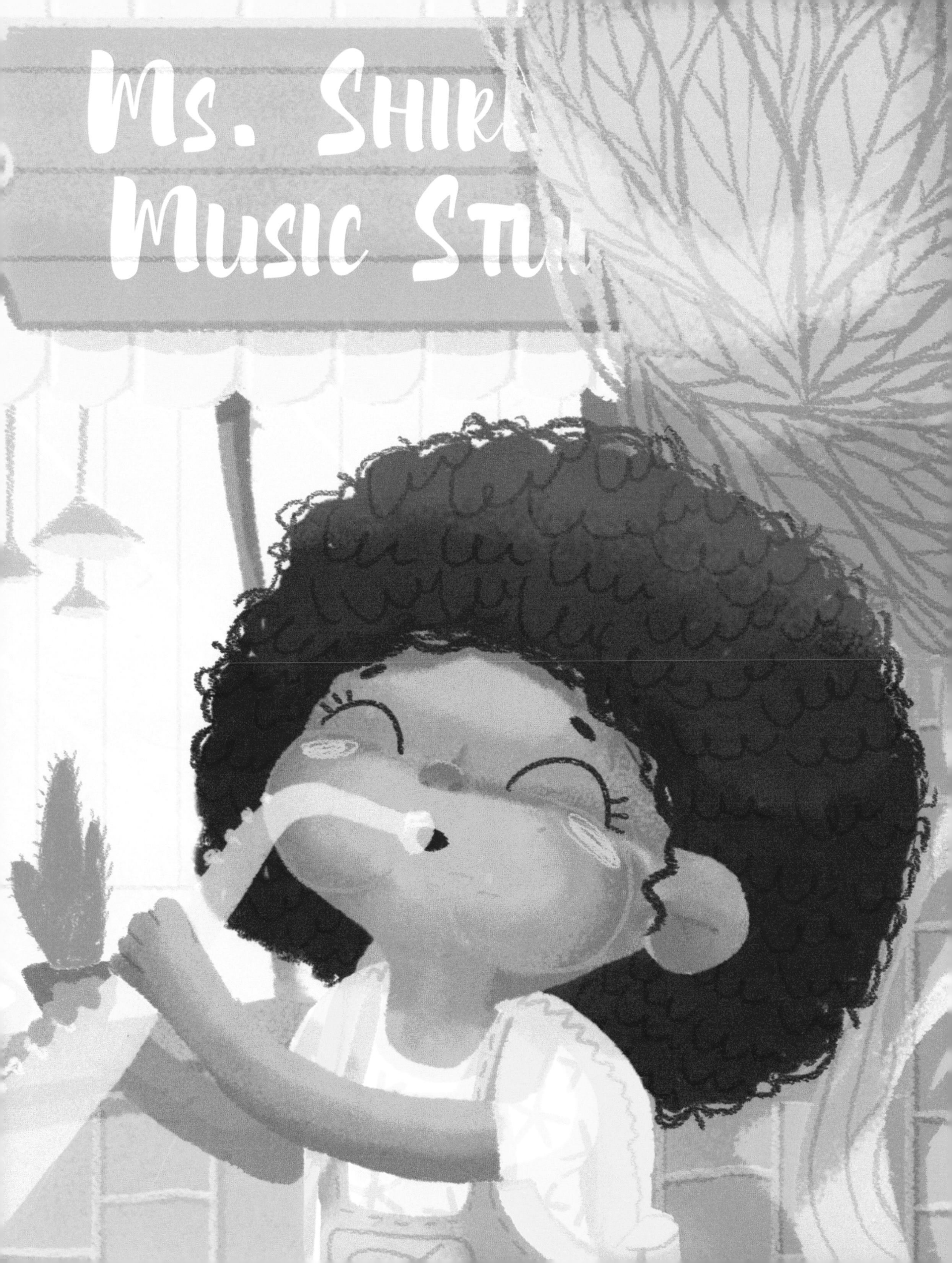
Ms. Shir
Music Stu

"Hi, Ms. Shirley!"
Martine yelled

Martine slapped the window and waved with both hands.

Now you may not know this, but Martine loves peaches! She loves to feel the fuzzy skin and taste the sweet-sweet juice inside. Mr. Johnny's grocery had peaches so big you needed to hold them with two hands.

Mr. Johnny's
Grocery Shop

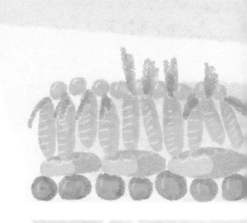

"Hi, Mr. Johnny"
SHOUTED MARTINE.

Peaches

Ba

MR. JOHNNY WAS SO STARTLED HE TOSSED HIS APPLES INTO THE AIR!

LATER THAT DAY, THE RAIN OUTSIDE WAS SCARY!

Martine's mom came to pick her up early from school.

"We're taking a surprise trip to Grandma's," she said. "Daddy is going to meet us there."

On the drive to Grandma's...

The heavy rain sounded like static – Psssssshhh!

Lightning flashed in the sky as if someone was playing with a big light switch!

The wind blew so fast trees looked like they would be snatched out of the ground!

And thunder shook the Earth as if giants were jumping nearby.

When they arrived at grandma's, Martine had to take a bath. Then, her dad pulled her favorite crocodile 'blankie' out of his suitcase and wrapped her up in it. The family rushed to the living room as grandma clicked on the news. There was a terrible storm on TV:

"Hurricane Willis is bringing a lot of rain," said the reporter.

"THAT'S OUR HOUSE!"
MARTINE YELLED.

Once it was safe to go home, Martine's neighborhood wasn't as she remembered. The sweet smells, pretty colors and beautiful music had disappeared.

For days, people stood around sad looking at their houses and shops. Until one afternoon Martine got an idea!

The next morning,
Martine jumped out of bed!

She wiggled into her school clothes!

She brushed her teeth in a flash!

She gobbled up her breakfast!

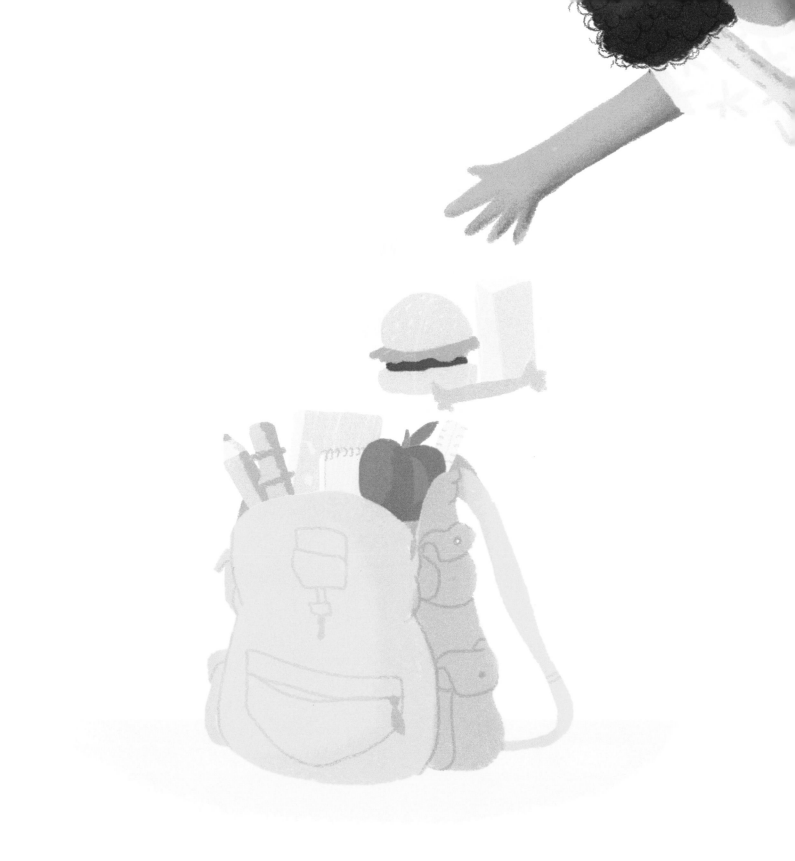

Swiped her lunch from the kitchen counter!

Then, she burst through the front door and looked up to the big blue sky.

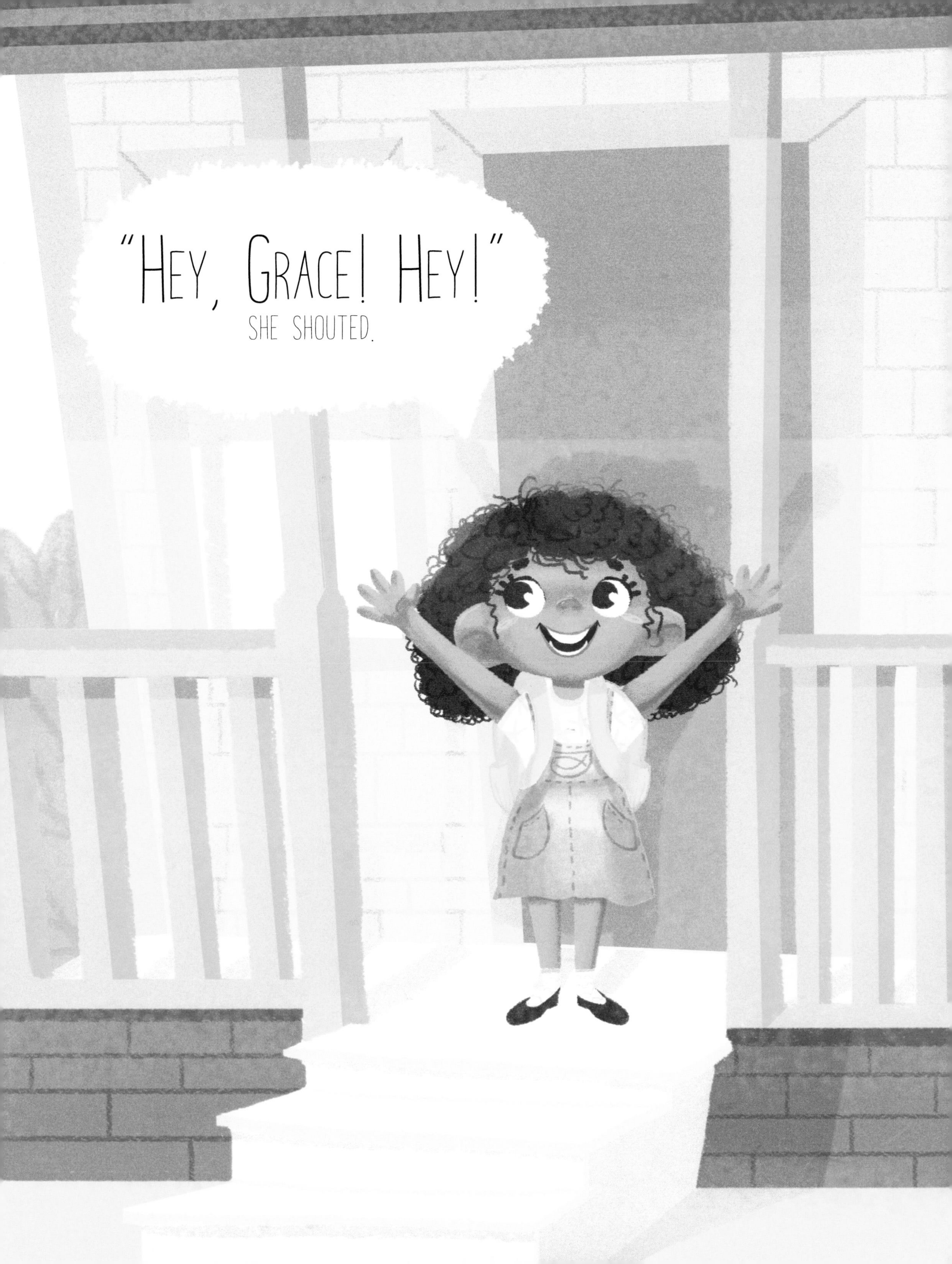

"HEY, GRACE! HEY!"
SHE SHOUTED.

Every morning Martine did this with the same excitement.

"Hey, Lisa girl!"

"Bonjour, Penelope"

"Ello, Jill!"

"Good day, Charlie!"

"HOLA, LUCA!"

"HI, DREW!"

One day, Mr. Johnny stopped Martine on her way to school and asked:

"MARTINE! Little girl,
who in the world
are you talking to?"

"People on TV named the rainy days 'Willis'.
Well, I want to name the sunny days too,"
Martine whispered.

Mr. Johnny looked like he'd seen a ghost. He reached behind him for his chair and plopped down. When people came to see if he was okay, Mr. Johnny told them what Martine said.

As Martine was skipping home from school that day something strange happened. People were sweeping dirt out of their shops, putting in new windows, painting store signs and carrying big bags of garbage out of their homes.

MARTINE HELPED WHERE SHE COULD!

Before long, their neighborhood looked better than before!

People threw a big party in the street to celebrate. Ms. Shirley's students played music with their new instruments. Mr. Pip baked a cake, long as a picnic table, covered with delicious frosting and purple sprinkles.

At the parade, Mr. Johnny walked up to Martine carrying the biggest peach she'd ever seen! It was so plump she had to hold it with two hands!

Martine danced holding her peach and smiling from ear to ear. People in her community found new joy and strength in each other and themselves.

JESSE BYRD
LOVES:

HIS WIFE, EMAAN.

WRITING STORIES

READING BOOKS

PLAYING VIDEO GAMES
AND WATCHING MOVIES

FRENCH TOAST

WARM POPCORN

Jesse Byrd is the international award-winning author of the children's book King Penguin. A fun-loving story about a penguin journeying across the sea and discovering who he is. Jesse believes everyone is given a special gift. Part of life's journey is to find it, take care of it, and use it to better the lives of other people.

Want to know a secret about Jesse?
He is an expert Milkshake-Maker!

www.jessebcreative.com
Instagram: @jessebcreative

Anastasiia Ku
LOVES:

CREATING NEW WORLDS

CHUBBY ANIMALS

PLAYING MUSIC

HER WONDERFUL LIFE

Harry Potter books

Anastasiia believes inside of every grown-up lives the child they once were.
She tries talking to these children through her illustrations, because she feels
the child inside each of us is capable of true magic!

Want to know a secret about Anastasiia?
She is absolutely the world's silliest runner! When Anastasiia runs she looks like
a hungry raccoon who just stole some yummy food from humans.

www.piclit.ru
Instagram: @piclit